I0823232

GOLF JOKES

DADS

514 KNEE-SLAPPERS FOR *the* 19TH HOLE

Jay Wallace

BLUESTONE
BOOKS

Putt-erly Hilarious Golf Jokes for Dads.

www.bluestonebooks.co

ISBN: 978-1-965636-18-3 (paper over board)

Printed in China

10 9 8 7 6 5 4 3 2 1

Project editor: Meaghan Cahill
Designer: Melissa Gerber

Chapter 1

COOL CLUB

CONTENTS

What's a golfer's favorite type of sandwich?

A club sandwich!

Why do golfers always carry an extra pair of socks?

In case they get a hole in one.

How do pro-golfers stay cool during a game?

They stand next to the fans.

Why should you trust a golfer's world view?

They always putt things in perspective.

Why are golfers so patient?

Because they know success comes one *stroke* at a time.

Where do golfers go on Saturday nights?

Out clubbing!

Why do golfers make great philosophers?

Because they're always pondering the course ahead.

What's the difference between a whiff and a practice swing?

No one curses after a practice swing.

How are golf balls like eggs?

They're white, sold by the dozen, and you're constantly having to buy more.

What's the difference between a golfer and a fisherman?

When a golfer lies, he doesn't have to bring anything home to prove it.

Golfers' Favorite Cocktails

Par-tini

Long Island Iced Tee

Club Soda

How did the golfer get the nickname 'the chef'?

He was slicing everything.

What do golfers do when they're struggling at golf?

Join the club.

What do you call a golfer who gets a lot of holes in one?

A one-hole wonder.

What's a golfer's favorite type of music?

Swing music.

What does a golfer eat?

They survive on nothing but greens.

Why did the golfer help build the playground?

He wanted to work on his swing.

What's a golfer's favorite game?

Golf! What did you expect—chess?

How many golfers does it take to change a tire?

Fore!

Why do golf courses get hot after tournaments?

Because all the fans leave.

Why are computers so good at golf?

Because they have a hard drive.

What do golfers do on their day off?

Putter around.

What's a golfer's favorite type of coffee?

They actually only drink tee.

What do golfers do if they want to go golfing on Election Day?

They make sure to cast an absent-tee ballot.

What's a golfer's favorite vegetable?

Green beans.

What is a golfer's least favorite vegetable?

Cabbage.

I used to feed the gorillas at my local zoo from a distance using a golf club...

I'd drive them bananas.

Where on the course do golfers like to drink?

The watering holes.

What did the golfer say when someone insulted him unnecessarily?

"That was a chip shot."

Why do golfers love donuts?

Because they're always looking for that hole-in-one.

What's a golfer's favorite bird?

Any birdie will do.

What do you get when you cross a baseball field with a golf course?

A diamond in the rough.

Why do golfers like tea parties?

The love the 'tee-time'!

Why did the golfer quit his job?

He wanted to drive around all day.

How is golf like fishing?

Both mysteriously encourage exaggeration.

Why did the golfer walk away angry?

He was really tee'd off.

Where are you most likely to find a bear on a golf course?

In the cub house.

Why did the golfer refuse to play cards?

He was afraid of a bad hand.

What's a golfer's favorite kind of workout?

Fore-arm curls.

How do golfers wish each other good luck?

"Hope you have a tee-rific day!"

What do you call a golf course that's always sunny?

A fairway paradise.

Why did the golfer join a band?

He wanted to improve his swing rhythm.

What's a golfer's favorite dance move?

The Bogey.

What's a golfer's favorite kind of potato?

A teeter-tot.

Why did the golf course get a new haircut?

It wanted to stay on the cutting edge.

What's a golfer's favorite pasta dish?

Quattro fore-maggi. It's a fore-cheese blend!

How does a golf dad discuss the facts of life with his kids?

He talks about the birdies and the tees.

What's a golfer's favorite bird?

Any birdie will do.

What type of beard is best for a golfer?

A goat-tee

What do golfers do at Christmas?

Decorate the tee.

What do you call the emcee at a major golf tournament?

The Masters of Ceremonies.

What did one golf glove say to the other?

Get a grip.

What did the golf ball say when it left?

Gotta roll.

When is a golfer like a toilet?

When he hits a flush.

What do you call a hot, lazy afternoon on the golf course?

A dogleg afternoon.

Why did the golfer bring a ladder?

To reach new heights with his clubs.

Why didn't the golfer want to do data entry?

It's tee-dious work.

“Putt It Like It’s Hot”

—Snoop Dogg

“Fairway to Heaven”

—Led Zeppelin

“Sweet Driver of Mine”

—Guns N’ Roses

“Eye of the Tiger Woods”

—Survivor

Chapter 2

TEE-RIFIC SKILLS

Why was the golfer so good at math?

Because he always knew how to subtract strokes.

Why do golfers make great detectives?

They always follow through on their leads.

How do golfers stay calm during stressful rounds?

They keep their cool under par-sure.

Who are the quickest learners when it comes to golf?

Tee-nagers.

My golf game is like a mystery novel...

Full of unexpected twists and hazards.

What's the easiest shot in golf?

Your fourth putt.

If I had a dollar for every time I missed a putt, I'd be driving a new car!

What's the easiest way to hook a ball?

Try to slice it.

Why don't golfers ever argue?

They always aim for common ground.

Golf is the perfect thing to do on a Sunday because you spend more time praying on the course than if you went to church.

How do you teach a golfer to box?

Tell him to take a swing.

Why don't golfers ever get lost?

They always follow the course.

How do golfers like their eggs?

Scrambled.

What weapon does a terrible golfer carry?

A shank.

What do you get when you cross a short golf shot with a person living in a monastery?

A chip-monk.

What's one rule all golfers should follow to improve their game?

Go back in time and start playing at a younger age.

The only time a golfer drives straight is on the golf course—and even that's rare!

Why couldn't Tiger Woods listen to music?

He broke all the records.

What did the golf pro say to his student?

Keep your head down and your drive up!

Which seats do golfers reserve at a show?

The front nine.

Why don't golfers ever fight?

They prefer to settle things on the fairway.

I'm on a whiskey diet—I've lost three strokes already!

What do you call a golfer who only likes his team when they're winning?

A fair-way fan.

Who's the best person at the golf course to make coffee?

The groundskeeper.

What do golfers do on a farm?

Put the cart before the horse.

What's the difference between a bad golfer and a bad skydiver?

Golfers go WHACK..."Damn" and skydivers go "Damn"...WHACK.

Why didn't the golfer make firm plans?

He liked to keep things up in the air.

What do you call a golfer who's always stealing shiny equipment?

A club-tomanac.

What do you use to find the location of a golf ball?

A lie detector.

Did you hear about the golfer who didn't have metal clubs in his bag?

He was iron deficient.

Golf is a lot like taxes: You go for the green and come out in the hole.

What do you get when you cross a funny golfer with a rubbery toy?

Silly Putter-y

Did you hear about the golfer whose clubs burst into flames?

He had a few irons in the fire.

What did the guy get when he threw his club into the air?

A birdie.

Golf is an odd game: You hit down to make the ball go up; you swing left and the ball goes right; the lowest score wins; and on top of that, the winner buys the drinks.

What do you call a golf swing from a pantsless player?

A moon shot.

What do you call someone who can drink and golf at the same time?

A multi-flasker.

Why did the golfer stay up all night before playing a round of golf?

He misunderstood the saying, *You snooze, you lose.*

Golf: the art of turning a beautiful walk into a frustrating game.

Snacks for All Eighteen Holes

Putt-tarts

Chocolate Chip Cookies

Fore-itos

Donut Holes

Mac and Tees

Golf is the only game where the ball lies poorly and the golfers lie well.

Why did the fortune teller play golf?

To get fore-sight.

Why did the golf ball go to school?

To master the course.

Why do golfers work in marketing?

They can put a good spin on anything.

What does it sound like when a golf ball laughs?

Tee-hee, tee-hee, tee-hee.

Why was the golf club always calm?

It knew how to handle the pressure.

Chapter 3

FAIRWAY FOOLISHNESS

How can a ball hit farthest from the hole be USGA quality?

When USGA stands for "U Suck, Go Again."

Golfer A: "The problem with your game is your loft."

Golfer B: "My loft?"

Golfer A: "Lack of Freaking Talent."

What are the four worst words you could hear during a game of golf?

It's still your turn.

A man fell into a bin of discount clubs at the pro shop. Doctors said he'll be okay, but he's not out of the woods yet.

What do you call a golfer who tells dad jokes?

A pun-derful companion.

One player asked, "Were you really *under* the whole day?"

The other answered, "Yes...under a tree... under a bush...and under the water."

Why do golfers hate cake?

Because they just get slices.

What did the angry golfer say?

Kiss my putt!

When is it too wet to play golf?

When your golf cart capsizes.

What did you get on your last hole?

Depressed.

Cars Golfers Love to Drive

Caddy-lac

Driving Range Rover

Model-Tee Fore-d

Dune Bogy

Why did the golfer always carry a spare tire?

In case he needed a little extra drive.

What do you call a golfer with a PhD?

A hackademic.

One player asked,

"Do you play off scratch?"

The other player replied,

"I sure do. Every time I hit the ball, I scratch my head and wonder where it went."

Why do golfers hate the wind?

Because it gives them a rough time.

What should NASA do if they want to explore water on Mars?

Send a bad golfer there.

What's a golfer's favorite haircut?

A fade.

Golfer: "Please stop checking your watch all the time. It's distracting!

Caddy: "This isn't a watch, it's a compass."

What do you call a bad day of golf?

A rough day.

Why did the golfer bring a band-aid?

For his cut shot.

Why did the golfer bring string to the course?

To tie up loose ends in their game.

What's a golfer's worst enemy?

A squirrel with a golf ball collection.

What is the difference between put and putt?

Put means to place a thing where you want it; and a putt is a futile attempt to do the same thing.

What do you get when you cross a golfer's pants with a chocolate snack?

A Knickers bar.

Why are golfers terrible at poker?

They can't help but fold under pressure.

If you think it's hard to meet new people, pick up the wrong ball on a golf course.

Why did the golfer get a speeding ticket?

Because he was caught driving on the green.

What did the golfer say to the ball after he struck it?

"Fore-give me!"

Why did the golfer go to jail?

Because he shot a birdie and an eagle.

What is it called when golfers urinate on a golf course?

A tee-pee.

How do golfers get their numbers mixed up?

They shoot a six, yell "fore!", and write five.

How can you tell that someone is a bad golfer?

They have to get their ball retriever re-gripped more often than their clubs.

Why are mini golf players depressed?

Because they have no drive.

What is the only sport that's four letters and starts with a 't'?

Golf.

What do you call an itchy person who can shoot a par or better?

A scratch golfer.

Why did the golfer bring a first-aid kit?

He kept getting hurt feelings from all the bogeys.

What do you call an angry golfer?

Teed off!

What race do golfers love to compete in?

An Ironman competition.

Did you hear about the golfer who used to wear colorful pants?

He had a checkered past.

What do you call a story that involves golfers and spies?

Stroke and dagger.

What do you get when you cross a golf ball that lands in a pond with a Deep Purple song?

Stroke on the water.

What area of the fairway is a dog's favorite?

The ruff.

What do you call a police van filled with golfers' assistants?

A caddy wagon.

Why did the golfer cross the road?

To get to the other tee.

Did you hear about the politician who's working twice as hard?

He played thirty-six holes of golf.

What do you call it when someone leaves the scene of a golf cart accident?

A bump and run.

Where is the lie in golf?

On the scorecard.

Did you hear about the actor who took too many strokes on the golf course?

He wasn't right for the par.

What do you call a golfer retrieving a ball in deep water?

A scuba driver.

Three golf clubs walk into a bar. The putter orders a beer, and the pitching wedge orders a gin & tonic. When the barman asks the third club if he wants anything, he replies, "No thanks, I'm the driver."

What should you do if your round of golf is interrupted by a lightning storm?

Walk around holding your 1-iron above your head because even Mother Nature can't hit a 1-iron.

One golfer asked another: "Do you think my golfing is improving?"

The other golfer replied: "Yes, you miss a lot closer now."

Golf is a game of chance where you can hit a 2-acre fairway 10 percent of the time and a 2-inch branch 90 percent of the time.

Why did the golfer plant grass in his living room?

He wanted a home green advantage.

I've just invented a new golf ball that will go in the hole if it gets within four inches. Note to self: Do NOT put ball in back pocket.

What's a golfer's favorite chore?

Iron-ing.

Did you hear about the golfer who was so nervous about the tournament that he threw up?

I suppose it's just barf for the course.

What's a beginner golfer's favorite exercise?

The swing and miss.

Why did the golfer take a pencil to the course?

To draw a better score.

What do you call a golfer with no clubs?

Pointless.

What did the golfer get when she lost her golf ball?

A hole-in-none.

What's a golfer's favorite type of humor?

Par-ody

Golfer: "The doctor says I can't play golf."

Caddy: "Oh, he's played with you, too?"

What did the golf ball say to the hole?

I'm just here to drop in for a visit.

What did the golf ball say to the driver?

"You really know how to take me for a ride."

Where does a golfer head in an emergency?

To the bunker.

Golf is a game invented by God to punish people who retire early.

Why don't golfers ever play hide-and-seek?

They're always finding themselves in the rough.

What kind of tree loves golf?

A tee-tree.

What did the public golf course say to the private one?

"I'm green with envy."

If Golf Had
Animal Mascots
Tee-gers
Birdies
Caddy-cats
Putterflies
Eagles
E

What do you call a golf club that sings?

A pitch-perfect driver.

What's a golfer's favorite type of comedy?

Stand-up clubs.

What did one golf ball say to another golf ball?

"See you round."

Why are golf balls great singers?

They're never flat.

What is the difference between a golfer and a skydiver?

A skydiver has a better chance of landing in a fairway.

Chapter 4

FAME OF THE GAME

What did Shakespeare say when asked to play another round?

"To tee, or not to tee, that is the question."

Why did the golfer call his partner's ball 'Captain Kirk'?

Because it went where no ball has gone before.

What do you call a skeleton's second chance shot?

A skull-igan.

Why couldn't the monster become a pro golfer?

He was a bogeyman.

Where do zombies play golf?

On the golf corpse.

Why couldn't Cinderella play golf?

Because she always runs away from the ball.

What did Nat King Cole sing after he won a round of golf?

"Un-fore-gettable, in every way."

Which actress is incredible at golf?

Minnie Driver.

What is Maleficent's favorite golf accessory?

A witching wedge.

What's a golfer's favorite superhero?

Iron Man.

What did Master Yoda say when Luke sliced the ball onto the next fairway?

May the Fores be with you.

What two places have the most curses?

An ancient tomb and a golf course.

What movie about golf took place in a galaxy far, far away?

Par Wars.

What fabled character holds his golf club tightly?

Grip Van Winkle.

What do you get when you cross a shallow pit with a golfing comedian?

Adam Sand Trap-ler.

How did Moses prove that he was a good golfer?

He parred the Red Sea.

What do you call a popular *Sesame Street* character who takes one swing less than a par?

Big Birdie.

What do you get when you cross a cereal box character with one of golf's all-time greats?

Tony the Tiger Woods.

Which British actor uses only metal golf clubs?

Jeremy Irons.

Which TV show featured a mother and five kids who loved to golf?

The Par-tridge Family.

"I Will Survive (The Sand Trap)"

—Gloria Gaynor

"Don't Stop Believin' (In the Birdie)"

—Journey

"All About That Ace"

—Meghan Trainor

"Rolling in the Green"

—Adele

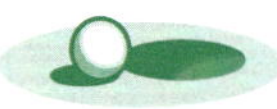

What do you get when you cross a funny movie about golf with Donald Duck?

Caddy-quack!

Who do you get when you cross a curving golf shot with a rapper?

Vanilla Slice.

What do you get when you cross an extreme golf shot with a pirate?

Captain Hook-ed.

What kind of patterned sweaters do pirates wear on a golf course?

Argh-yle.

Which ancient Egyptian pharaoh liked to golf?

King Putt.

What skating performance features bad golfers?

The Slice-capades.

Did you hear about the golfer whose shot landed in a music store?

He broke three records.

What do you call a female popstar who keeps missing her shots?

Taylor Whiffed.

What do you get when you cross a golfer with Humphrey Bogart's stand-in?

A double Bogey.

What do you call a wizard who can turn himself into a golf club?

Harry Putter.

Other Things Golfers Do

Watch Tee-V

Catch a Drive-in Movie

Play Caddy Land

Go to Par-ties

What do you call a golf shot that ends up in outer space?

A black hole in one.

What is Michael Corleone's advice to golfers?

"Keep your friends close, but your nine iron closer."

Which *Star Wars* character was good at sinking short shots?

Jabba the Putt.

Why did Tarzan spend so much time on the golf course?

He was perfecting his swing.

Did you hear that the sandwich shop in town added a mini-golf course?

I tried it out, but it was sub-par.

Why do golf announcers whisper?

They don't want to wake the people watching.

What is it called when you hit a ball from Miami to Guadalajara?

The Golf of Mexico.

Did you hear about the golfer whose clubs burst into flames?

Everyone said he was on fire.

What do you get when you cross a golf club with a classic band?

Fleetwood Mac.

What do you call a spy who loves golf?

Double Bogey O Seven.

What do you get when you cross a golf vehicle with a famous musician?

Paul McCartney.

What is a golfer's favorite *Star Wars* character?

Luke Skyputter.

What do you call an old golfer who tells jokes?

Tee Martin.

What do you call a golfer who solves mysteries?

Sherlock Holes

Which actress got a second chance at success?

Carey Mulligan.

Where do golfers vacation?

Club Med.

Who's a golfer's favorite pirate?

Captain Jack Par-row.

What do you call a golfing vampire?

Count Putt-ula.

What's a golfer's favorite cartoon character?

Putter Pan.

What's a golfer's favorite board game?

Par-cheesi.

What did the rapper Chamillionaire say when he came in a stroke under par?

"Tryna catch me ridin' birdie!"

Why don't turtles play golf?

Because they like cricket better.

What's a golfer's favorite game show?

Wheel of Fore-tune.

What's a golfer's favorite video game?

Fore-tnite

What do you call a golf club that tells stories?

A fairway yarn!

If Golfers Were Scriptwriters

"May the course be with you."

(Star Wars)

"You had me at hole-in-one."

(Jerry Maguire)

"I feel the need...the need for tees!"

(Top Gun)

"You can't handle the putt!"

(A Few Good Men)

"Drive long and prosper."

(Star Trek)

"Houston, we have a bogey."

(Apollo 13)

Why do golfers love geometry?

Because they're always working on their angles.

What is it called when a golfer makes a comparison?

A meta-fore.

Why does Sir-Mix-a-Lot always chip the ball away from the flagstick?

He likes big putts and he cannot lie.

Chapter 5

GOLF ACCORDING TO GOLFERS

"I have a tip that will take five strokes off anyone's golf game. It's called an eraser."

—Arnold Palmer

"While playing golf today, I hit two good balls. I stepped on a rake."

—Henry Youngman

"If you drink, don't drive. Don't even putt."

—Dean Martin

"It took me seventeen years to get three thousand hits in baseball. It took one afternoon on the golf course."

—Hank Aaron

Steven Spiel-bogey

Kim Par-dashian

Brad Putt

Al Green

Ice Slice

Leonardo Drive-Caprio

Bogey-oncé

Sammy Divot Jr.

**“We learn so many things from golf—
how to suffer for instance.”**

—Bruce Lansky

**“If you watch a game, it’s fun.
If you play at it, it’s recreation.
If you work at it, it’s golf.”**

—Bob Hope

**“Pressure is when you play $5 a
hole with only $2 in your pocket.”**

—Lee Trevino

**“The income tax has made more liars
out of American people than golf has.”**

—Will Rogers

"Give me fresh air, a beautiful partner, and a nice round of golf, and you can keep the fresh air and the round of golf."

—Jack Benny

"Golf is a game invented by the same people who think music comes out of a bagpipe."

—Lee Trevino

"I don't say my golf game is bad, but if I grew tomatoes, they'd come up sliced."

—Arnold Palmer

"If you are going to throw a club, it is important to throw it ahead of you, down the fairway, so you don't have to waste energy going back to pick it up."

—Tommy Bolt

"If a lot of people gripped a knife and fork as poorly as they do a golf club, they'd starve to death."

—Sam Snead

"I know I am getting better at golf because I am hitting fewer spectators."

—Gerald Ford

"Golf is a good walk spoiled."

—Mark Twain

"Golf tips are like aspirin. One may do you good, but if you swallow the whole bottle, you will be lucky to survive."

—Harvey Penick

"I play golf with friends sometimes, but they are never friendly games."

—Ben Hogan

"The only sure rule in golf is he who has the fastest golf cart never has to play the bad lie."

—Mickey Mantle

Film Classics: Golf Edition

West Course Story

Vir-tee-go

The Outdrivers

Ben-Par

Sense and Putt-sibility

The Wolf of Ball Street

The Breakfast Club

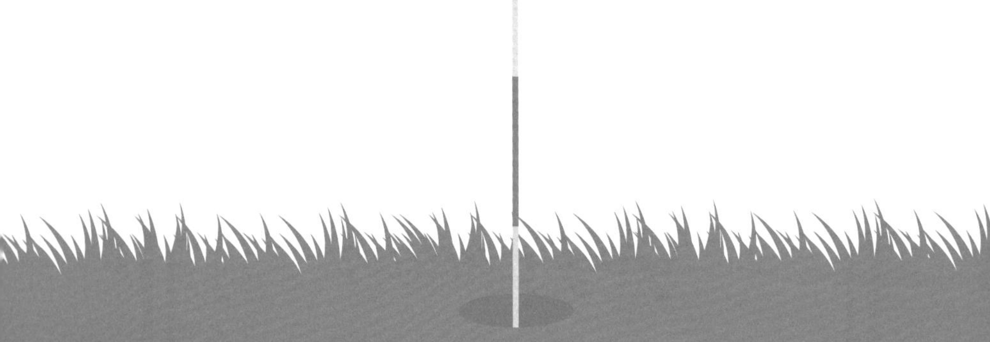

Chapter 6

LONG GAME

James was playing a round of golf with the club pro one day, and after 18 holes they went into the clubhouse. James asked the pro: "What did you think of my game?"

The pro replied: "You should shorten your clubs by one inch."

James asked if the pro thought this would help his game.

To which the pro said, "No! It will help them fit in the trash can!"

A guy on vacation finishes his round and goes into the clubhouse. The head pro asks, "Did you have a good time out there?"

The man replies, "Fabulous, thank you." "Good to hear," says the pro.

"How did you find the greens?"

"Easy," says the man, "I just walked to the end of the fairways and there they were."

Steve had tried to be particularly careful about his language as he played golf with his preacher. But on the 12th hole, when he twice failed to hit out of a sand trap, he lost his resolve and let fly with a string of expletives. The preacher felt obliged to respond. "I have observed," he said in a calm voice, "that the best golfers do not use foul language."

"I guess not," said Steve, "what the hell do they have to bitch about?"

Noting that her husband looked more haggard and disgruntled than usual after his weekly golf game, his wife asked what was wrong. He answered, "Well, on the 4th hole, Harry had a heart attack and died. It was terrible! The entire rest of the day, it was hit the ball, drag Harry, hit the ball, drag Harry!"

A fellow caddy and I recently helped two older men around our course. Failing yet again to get the ball in the air, the worst golfer of the pair exclaimed, "I suppose you have never seen any player worse than me?"

My friend the caddy replied, "There are plenty worse than you sir, but they all quit playing years ago."

Four guys who worked together always golfed at 7 a.m. on Sunday. When someone transferred to another office, they showed up on Sunday looking to fill out the foursome. A woman standing near the tee said, "Hey, I like to golf. Can I join the group?"

They were hesitant but said she could come once to try it. She said, "Good, I'll be there at 6:30 or quarter to seven." She showed up right at 6:30 and wound up setting a course record with a 7-under-par round. The guys went nuts and everyone in the clubhouse congratulated her. Meanwhile, she was fun and pleasant the entire round. The guys happily invited her back the next week and she said, "Sure, I'll be here at 6:30 or quarter to 7."

Again, she showed up at 6:30 Sunday morning. Only this time, she played left-handed and matched her 7-under par score of the previous week. By now the guys were totally amazed, and asked her to join the group for keeps.

They had a beer after their round, and one of the guys asked her, "How do you know if you're going to golf right-handed or left-handed?"

She said, "That's easy. Before I leave for the golf course, I pull the covers off my husband, who sleeps in the nude. If his penis is pointing to the right, I golf right-handed; if it's pointed to the left, I golf left-handed."

One of the guys asked, "What if it's pointed straight up?"

She said, "Then I'll be here closer to 9 a.m.."

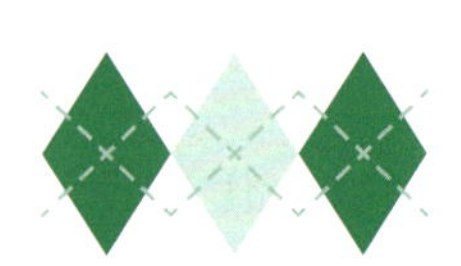

Classic Lit-tee-ra-ture

Harry Putter and the Deathly Holes

Nineteen Eighty-Fore

The Catcher in the Club

The Drive Also Rises

To Kill a Mocking-Birdie

John and Bob were two of the bitterest rivals at the club. Neither man trusted the other's arithmetic. One day they were playing a heated match and watching each other like hawks. After holing out on the 4th green and marking his six on the scorecard, John asked Bob, "What'd you have?"

"Six!" he answered and then hastily corrected himself—"No, no...a five."

Calmly, John marked the scorecard, saying out loud, "Eight!"

"Eight?" Bob exclaimed. "I couldn't have had eight."

John said, "Nope, you claimed six, then changed it to five, but actually you had seven."

"Then why did you mark down eight?" asked Bob.

John told him, "One-stroke penalty, for improving your lie."

Nick and Lou head out for a quick round of golf. Since they're short on time, they decide to play only nine holes. Nick says to Lou, "Let's say we make the time worth the while, at least for one of us, and spot $5 on the lowest score for the day."

Lou agrees and they enjoy a great game. After the 8th hole, Lou is ahead by one stroke, but he slices his ball into the rough on the 9th. "Help me find my ball; go look over there," he says to Nick.

After three minutes, neither has any luck. Since a lost ball carries a two-stroke penalty, Lou pulls a ball from his pocket and tosses it to the ground. "I've found my ball!" he announces triumphantly.

Nick looks at him forlornly, "After all the years we've been friends, you'd cheat me on golf for a measly five bucks?"

"What do you mean cheat? I found my ball sitting right here!"

"And a liar, too!" Nick says with amazement. "I'll have you know I've been standing on your ball for the last three minutes!"

A golfer sliced a ball into a field of chickens, striking one of the hens and killing it instantly. He was understandably upset and sought out the farmer. "I'm sorry," he said, "my terrible tee-shot hit one of your hens and killed it. Can I replace the hen?"

"I don't know about that," replied the farmer, mulling it over. "How many eggs a day do you lay?"

A bartender tried to cheer up a golfer by saying, "Well, something must have gone right in your game. Was there at least one hole with a bright spot?"

"Actually, the 4th hole was the best part of the day," the golfer recalled.

"I bet you had mad skills on at least that hole. What happened?"

"I lost my scoring pencil," the golfer cry-laughed.

A young man is trying to squeeze in nine holes before heading home. As he is about to tee off, an old gentleman shuffles onto the tee and asks if he can join him. He's worried the man will slow him down, but lets him join anyway.

When they reach the 9th fairway, the young man is facing a tough shot. A large pine tree sits in front of his ball, directly between it and the green. After several minutes of pondering how to hit the shot, the old man says, "You know, when I was your age, I'd hit the ball right over that tree." With the challenge before him, the young man swings hard, hits the ball, watches it fly into the branches, rattle around, and land with a thud a foot from where it had started.

"Of course," says the old man, "when I was your age, that tree was only three feet tall."

A golfer was having a terrible round—20-over par for the front nine with a bunch of balls lost in the water or rough. When his caddie let out a cough just as he was steadying himself over a 12-inch putt on the 10th, he lost it.

"You've got to be the worst caddie in the world!" he yelled.

"I doubt it," replied the caddie. "That would be too much of a coincidence."

Travel Destinations for Golfers
Par-celona
Ball-i
Mal-drives

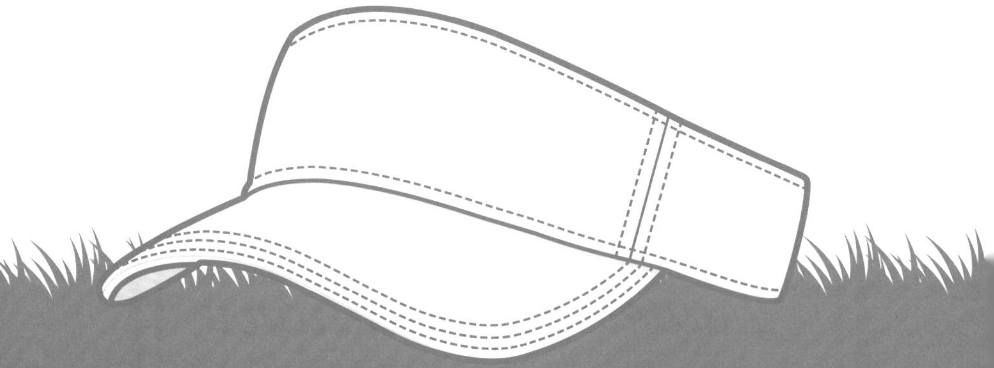

Chapter 7

PAR-FECT MATCH

**Golf is an easy game.
It's just hard to play.**

What did the wife say about her husband's golf obsession?

"It's driving a wedge between us!"

How is golf like marriage?

You start with high hopes
and end up in the rough.

Best Places to Meet Fellow Golfers

At a Ball

Book Club Meetings

Volun-tee-ring

Martin and his wife Debbie walk into a dentist's office. Martin says to the dentist, "Doc, I'm in one heck of a hurry. I have three buddies sitting out in my car waiting for us to play golf, so forget about the anesthetic, I don't have time for the gums to get numb. I just want you to pull the tooth and be done with it! Today's Friday and we have a 10:00 a.m. tee time at the best golf course in town. It's already 9:15."

The dentist thought to himself, *My goodness, this is surely a very brave man asking to have a tooth pulled without using anything to kill the pain.* So, the dentist asked Martin, "Which tooth is it, Sir?"

Martin turned to his wife and said, "Open your mouth and show him, dear..."

A couple has just gotten married. As they are retreating to the bedroom for the first time, the husband looks deeply into his wife's eyes and said, "Honey, I've got something to tell you. I haven't been completely honest. I am a golfing addict and every chance I get I'm going to go and have a round."

"OK," replied his wife. "As we are confessing, I haven't been completely honest with you, either. I'm a hooker."

"That's OK," said the husband. "You've just gotta make sure you keep your left arm straight and your head down longer."

A husband and wife are teeing off on the 7th hole. The husband slices his drive into the rough, with his line to the green blocked by a maintenance shed. He says to his wife, "I guess I'll take a drop."

The wife replies, "Wait, if we open the shed doors on both sides, you can hit straight through." He decides to try, but once again he doesn't hit it cleanly. The ball hits the shed and bounces back, hitting the wife in the head and seriously injuring her.

Fast forward a year, husband is back on the 7th tee with a friend and once again, slices his drive behind the shed. Just like his wife, the friend suggests opening the shed doors and hitting through. The husband replies, "I tried that exact shot last year and ended up taking triple bogey."

What does a golfer like to hear from his wife?

"Talk birdie to me."

What's the difference between the g-spot and a golf ball?

A guy will spend ten minutes trying to find his lost golf ball.

"I came home to my wife in lingerie. She said I could tie her up and do whatever I wanted, so I tied her to the chair and went to the driving range."

I told my buddy I got a new set of clubs for my wife. He said, "Sounds like a good trade!"

Golf is like marriage: If you take yourself seriously it won't work... and both are very expensive.

After the honeymoon, the new wife tells her husbands, "I think it's time for you to stop playing golf. In fact, you might as well sell all your clubs."

The husband replies, "You're starting to sound like my ex-wife."

His wife says, "I thought you said you've never been married before?"

The husband answers back, "I haven't."

Nick was in trouble when he forgot his wedding anniversary. Molly, his wife, told him, "Tomorrow there better be something in the driveway for me that goes from zero to two hundred in two seconds flat." The next morning, Molly found a small package in the driveway. She opened it and found their last credit card bill.

Golf-Related Pickup Lines

How about grabbing two of your friends so we can play a foursome?

Your putt looks great in those jeans!

So, what's it going to be today: Stroke Play or Skins?

Are you looking for the fairway? Because coming back to my hotel is the only fair way for the evening to go.

I'm not a pro, but meeting you makes me a major winner.

Would you mind checking my scorecard for me? It seems like I am missing a number—yours.

Why are golfers good at relationships?

They know how to take one fore the team.

Why did the golfer go to therapy?

He had trouble controlling his mood swings.

What is a golfer's favorite flower?

Fore-get me nots.

How do you know a golfer is cheating on his wife?

He always puts his driver in the wrong place.

Love is like golf: It's all about the follow through.

Why don't golf clubs ever argue?

They're too busy having a ball.

Why did the golf ball break up with the club?

The club was driving it away.

What did the golf ball say to the tee?

"You're so supportive."

What's a golfer's idea of a perfect date?

Dinner and a drive-in movie.

"You spend too much time thinking about golf!" a wife said to her husband. "Do you even remember the day we got married?"

"Of course I do!" the husband exclaimed. "It was the same day I sank that 45-foot putt."

A couple whose passion had waned saw a marriage counselor and went through a number of appointments that brought little success. Suddenly, at one session the counselor grabbed the wife and kissed her passionately. "There," he said to the husband. "That's what your wife needs every day of the week."

"Well," replied the husband. "I can bring her in on weekdays, but Saturdays and Sundays are my golf days."

Three men gathered together for a round of golf on Mother's Day. The men were quite surprised at being "let out" for the day, and each wanted to know how the other got away from their wife.

The first man said: "I bought a dozen red roses for my wife, and she was so happy that she let me go."

The second man said: "I purchased a diamond ring for my wife, and she was so thrilled with me that she let me go."

The third man said: "I woke up this morning, rolled over, looked at my wife, and said to her, 'Golf course or intercourse,' and she said, 'Wear a sweater, it's cold outside.'"

What do a golf buddy and a golf shirt have in common?

They always have your back on the course.

Why did the golfer stay married?

He was determined to stay the course.

Why do golfers make the best lovers?

They know how to handle their strokes.

What did the golf course say to his lover?

"You drive me wild!"

Where do golfers go on their first date?

Out clubbing.

A man and his buddy are out playing golf at their usual course. Just as one of them is about to chip onto the green, he spots a long funeral procession passing by on the road running alongside the course. He pauses mid-swing, removes his cap, bows his head, and takes a moment of silence. His friend, moved by the gesture, says, "That's one of the most respectful things I've ever witnessed. You must be a truly compassionate person."

The man replies, "Well, we were married for thirty-five years."

Chapter 8

HOLE-IN-ONE-LINERS

Golf: a game invented to punish people who retire early.

I play in the low 80s: If it's hotter than that I won't play.

Golf: a five-mile walk punctuated with disappointments.

If your opponent can't remember if he shot a six or a seven on a hole, chances are he had an eight on it.

In primitive society, when native tribes beat the ground with clubs and yelled, it was called witchcraft; today, in civilized society, it's called golf.

Never buy a putter until you've seen how well you can throw it.

The higher the handicap of the golfer, the more likely it is that he'll be telling you what you should be doing to fix your game.

Golf brings out the three-year-old in us—we struggle to count past five.

Golf is what you play when you're too out of shape to play other sports.

The closest thing golfers get to a beach party is when they're stuck in a sand trap with their buddies.

It takes a serious amount of balls to golf like I do.

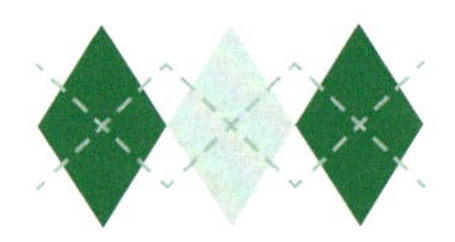

Obnoxious Things to Say...

When a swing takes the ball nowhere:

"The problem with your swing is obvious: You're standing way too close to the ball...*after* you've hit it."

After someone hits into a nasty rough:

"You're in Lion Country. If you find that ball, you're lyin'."

When someone makes a bad putt:

Careful there, putter fingers.

When you absolutely crush your drive straight down the middle of the fairway and outdrive your buddy by a lot: "I heard they're building a new super warehouse."

Buddy: "Oh, really? Where?"

You: "Between my ball and yours."

The game of golf is 90 percent mental and 10 percent mental.

A good golf partner is one who's always a little worse than you.

A "gimme" can best be defined as an agreement between two golfers, neither of whom can putt very well.

There is no game like golf: You go out with three friends, play eighteen holes, and return with three enemies.

Many golfers prefer a golf
cart to a caddy because it
cannot count, criticize, or laugh.

The most redundant thing
on a golf course is a ball-washer
on a hole with water hazards.

I'm not over the hill;
I'm just on the back nine.

Golfers aren't happy
unless they're teed off!

Golf forth and prosper.

I hate golf courses with too many trees.
I go to great links to avoid them.

It's easy to feel safe on a golf course
because there's always a doctor nearby.

Golfers' Favorite Shows

Iron Chef

Tee S. I.

How I Met Your Mulligan

The Caddymaid's Tale

Breaking Bad

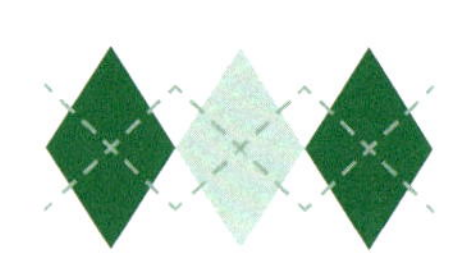

Trash Talk for Golfers

The way you play, you should put flags on the greens at half-mast.

I've seen better swings on a porch.

This guy spends more time in the sand than David Hasselhoff.

Sometimes the hardest thing about golf is being allowed out of the house to play it.

It's a strange world, isn't it? You hire someone to mow your lawn so that you'll have time to play golf for the exercise.

An interesting thing about golf is that no matter how badly you play, it's always possible to get worse.

If I hit it right, it's a slice. If I hit it left, it's a hook. If I hit it straight, it's a miracle.

The only problem with golf is that the slow groups are always in front of you and the fast groups are always behind you.

There are three ways to improve your golf game: Take lessons, practice constantly, or start cheating.

Real golfers have two vices: bragging and betting.

Real golfers don't cry when they line up their fourth putt.

Sorry, we don't give out par-ticipation trophies.

That golfer is so bad he brings flares, a compass, and emergency rations with him.

Life is full of challenges, but I'm just trying to stay on course.

I used to play golf, but I found it too rough.

I'm not a pro-golfer, but I do know how to have a tee-rrific time.

My putting game is like a magic trick: It disappears too often.

I'm always losing golf balls in the water—I guess you could say I have a sinking feeling about my game.

The only time I drive straight is on the golf course—and that's rare!

Golfers and their caddies always have a ball together.

I came for the golf, stayed for the sand traps.

Knock-Knock Golf Jokes

Knock, knock.
Who's there?
Boo.
Boo, who?
I'd cry too if I played golf like you.

Knock, knock.
Who's there?
Amy.
Amy, who?
Amy for the fairway—not the woods.

Knock, knock.
Who's there?
Noah.
Noah, who?
Noah golf pro who can fix your swing?

Knock, knock.
Who's there?
Wanda.
Wanda, who?
Wanda how deep your ball is in the lake.

Knock, knock.
Who's there?
Canoe.
Canoe, who?
Canoe hit one straight this time?

Knock, knock.
Who's there?
Annie.
Annie, who?
Annie-one know how many branches the golf ball hit as it entered the woods?

Golf and I have a love-hate relationship: I love it, and it hates me back.

Golfers are great at multi-tasking: They can swing and complain at the same time.

Golf is an endless series of tragedies obscured by the occasional miracle, followed by a good bottle of beer.

Golf is like life: full of missed opportunities and occasional glimpses of greatness.

The man who takes up golf to get his mind off his work soon takes up work to get his mind off golf.

Oxymoron: an easy par three.

Golf is harder than baseball—in golf you have to play your foul balls.

Golf is an expensive way of playing marbles.

Fairway: an unfamiliar tract of closely mown grass running directly from the tee to the green. Your ball can usually be found immediately to the left or right of it.

The only thing that causes more cheating than golf is the income tax.

Real golfers don't miss putts: They get robbed.

I'm not really that bad at putting; I just can't catch a break.

Golf is like life: You strive for the green but end up in the hole.

The best wood in most golfers' bags is the pencil.

A golf match is a test of your skill against your opponent's luck.

A golfer standing at a tee overlooking a river sees a couple of fishermen and says to his partner, "Look at those two idiots fishing in the rain."

Golfers, who claim they don't cheat, also lie.

The less skilled the player, the more likely he is to share his ideas about the golf swing.

The inevitable result of any golf lesson is the instant elimination of the one critical unconscious motion that allowed you to compensate for all your errors.

Everyone replaces his divot after a perfect approach shot.

Counting on your opponent to inform you when he breaks a rule is like expecting him to make fun of his own haircut.

An amateur golfer is one who addresses the ball twice: once before swinging, and once again after swinging.

Golf got its name because all the other four-letter words were taken.

Golfers who try to make everything perfect before taking the shot rarely make the perfect shot.

Never keep more than three hundred separate thoughts in your mind during your swing.

Since bad shots come in groups of three, a fourth bad shot is actually the beginning of the next group of three.

When your shot has to carry over a water hazard, you can either hit one more club or two more balls.

Golfers' Favorite Foods

Par-fait

Sandwedges

Birdie Nuggets

Mac 'n' Tees

Peanut Putter Cookies

Chapter 9

PUN AND DONE

You're a chip off the old block.

You've got to appeal to your putter judgement.

That's a load of trap!

Go fore it!

You never want to be the putt of the joke.

All bets par off.

I am the Golf-father.

I hit the ball as par as the eye can see.

To putt a long story short...

This is all fore the best.

I'm reviewing the course material.

Over the hills and fore away...

Money doesn't grow on tees.

Float like a butterfly, sting like a tee.

I golf you on my mind.

Putter late than never.

Seize every equal opportuni-tee.

It's a hole new game.

**I'd tell you a golf pun,
but it might go over par.**

I'm feeling a bit putt out.

**A lion would never play golf...
but a Tiger Wood.**

Time to par-tee!

Golf is my cup of tee.

A stroke of luck!

I'm feeling up to par.

My swing is un-fore-gettable.

I've got a fairway to go.

Fore-sight is key.

Green and bear it.

**When a golfer starts a band,
they call it a swing group.**

**I always bring my putter to the beach
because I can't resist the sand traps.**

**Golfers never retire;
they just lose their drive.**

**It's tough to iron out the details
when you're on the green.**

Live life on the putt-ing edge.

**When golfers eat fast food, they
order a club sandwich.**

Some golfers excel, while others just putter around.

Golfers are known to drive their point home, sometimes even 300 yards.

There's no iron-y in saying that golf is a sport of great course and effect.

Sometimes, golf is a matter of course; other times, it's just a matter of driving.

My golf game is rough, but I always find a way to wedge in some fun.

He's got the drive for success, but he still hasn't mastered his putt-entials.

I'm caught between a swing and a par'd place.

That new caddy really carried his weight. What a haul-in-one!

Don't be afraid to be honest about your golf game—no need for fairway-tales.

On the golf course, a miss-take is just par for the course.

A birdie in the hand is worth two in the bush.

Don't putt all your eggs in one basket.

A stitch in time saves nine holes.

Drive a hard bargain, but don't slice it.

The early birdie catches the warm.

When life gives you bunkers, make sandcastles.

The fairway to happiness is through a good game of golf.

Sometimes you just need to take a mulligan and give it another swing.

You miss 100 percent of the putts you don't take.

Golf: It's so ironic.

He's got fore-sight on and off the course.

If you want a hole-istic approach to health, play golf.

The grass isn't always greener on the other course.

If it ain't broke, try changing your grip.

It's surprisingly easy to hole a 50-foot putt when you lie 10.

The shortest distance between any two points on a golf course is a straight line that passes directly through the center of a very large tree.

The secret of good golf is to hit the ball hard, straight, and not too often.